He prayed one day to God that
if he could be successful he
would help Bless the world.

So the gentley hero came up with an idea
of selling mattress in his community.

And Mattress
Max The Helpin
Hero of Housto
Maxtress Max
Mattress's
Max's
Mattress
Own by
Mattress
Max

At this point the gently giant was known
to the community as Mattress Mac.

His heart always opened to poor out
aboundance of magical blessings to
people in need of major support.

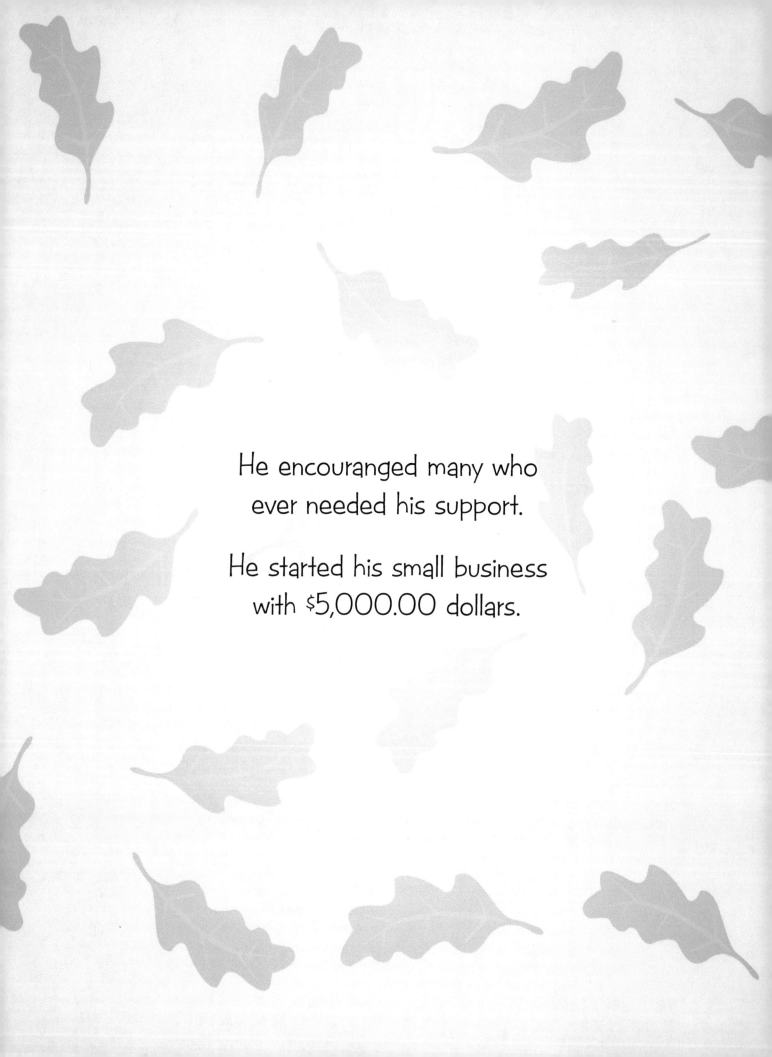

He encouranged many who
ever needed his support.

He started his small business
with $5,000.00 dollars.

He prayed Oh God show me the way.

God as I look out at the world help me to become a wonderful honest giving man. A man to help someone succeed in life such as I because through you God all things are possible.

Mattress Mac was up late one
night watching the 10:00 news.

He saw a mother of 6 being interviewed
on her stolen invention case.

She explained I have been working on
my invention case for over 9 years.

God blessed me with this invention.
The lady said I invented this machine
called a F.I.M.A. Word Scanner.

It is on the market as a Quickionary Pen.
A Invention company stole my idea.

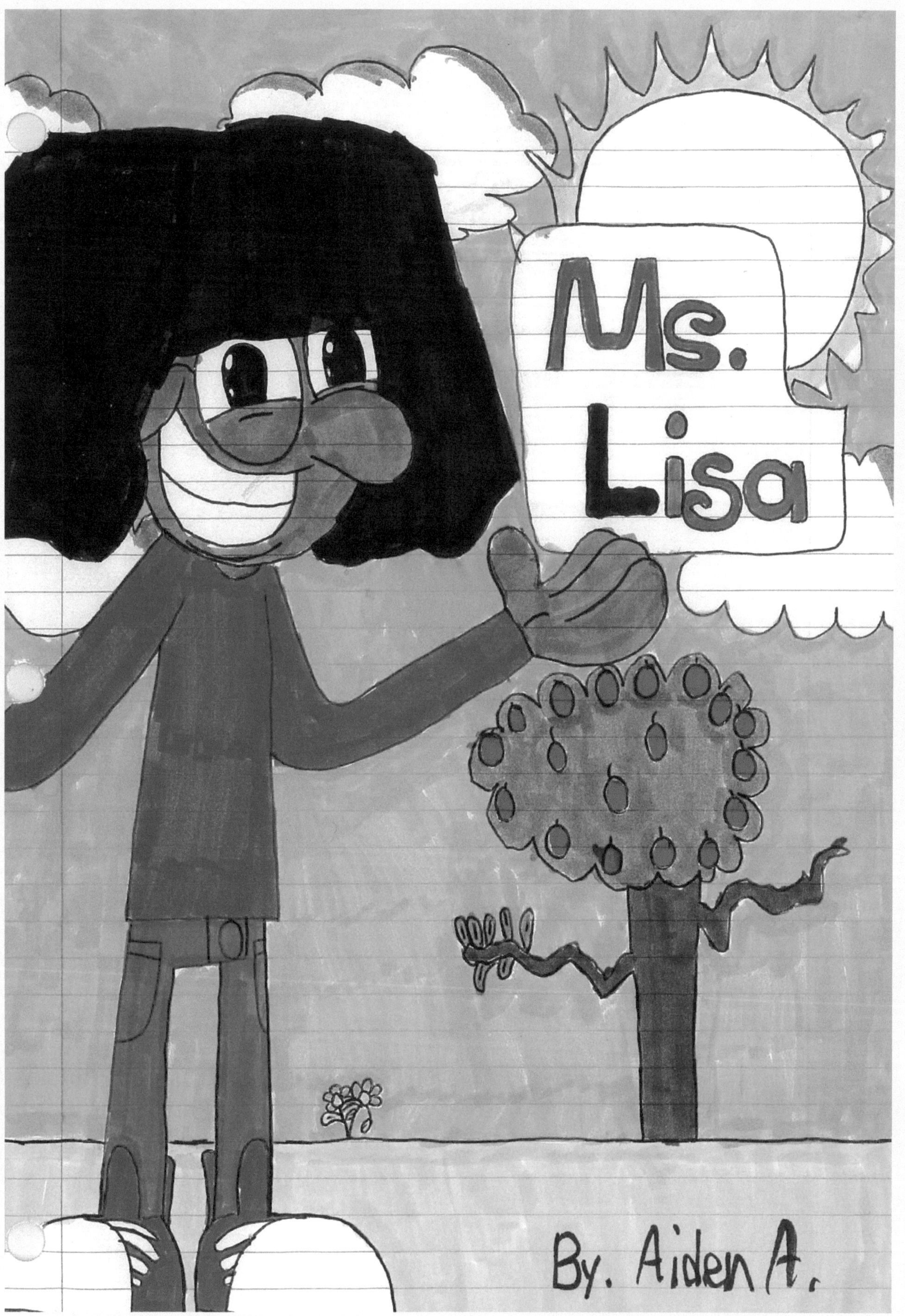
Ms.
Lisa
By. Aiden A.

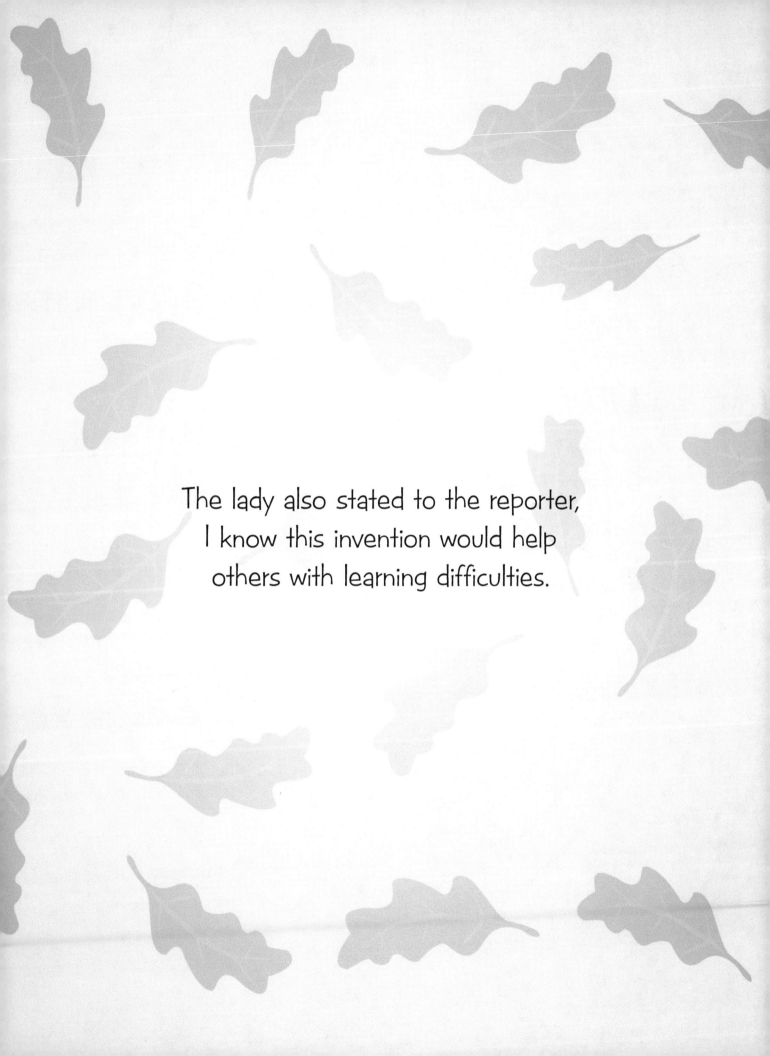

The lady also stated to the reporter,
I know this invention would help
others with learning difficulties.

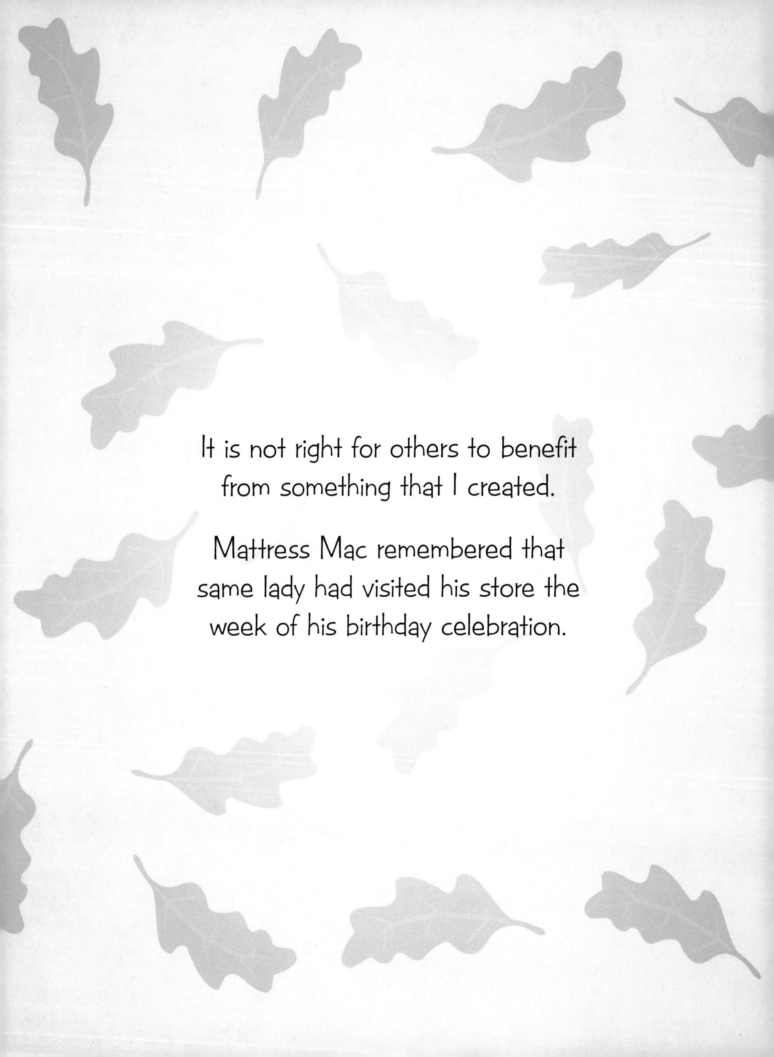

It is not right for others to benefit from something that I created.

Mattress Mac remembered that same lady had visited his store the week of his birthday celebration.

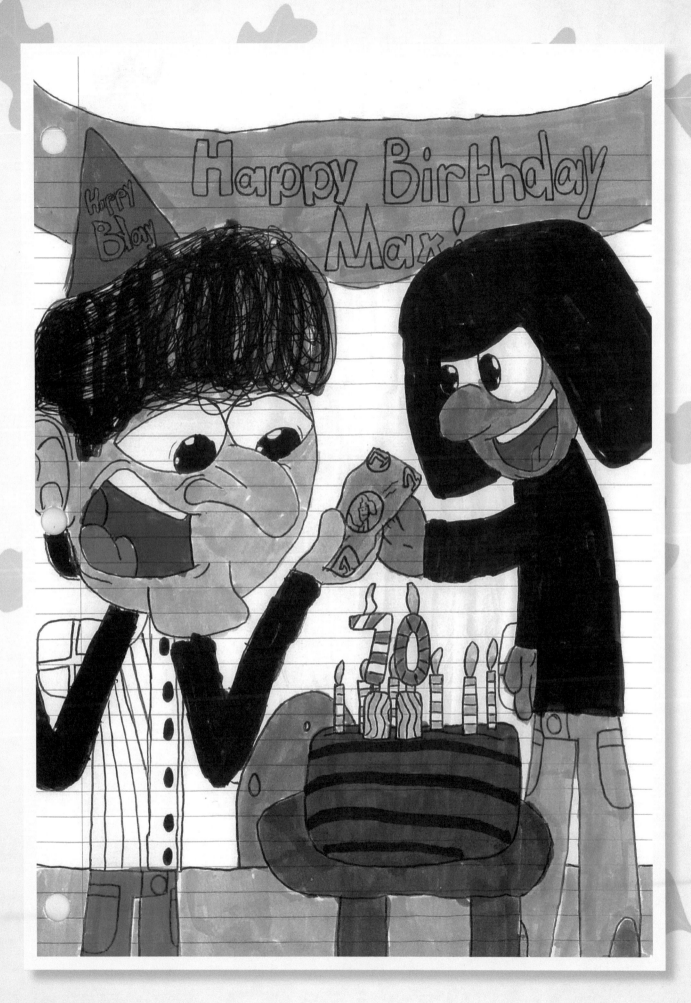

She said to him you are a great man. I wish
I could give you more but all I have is this
$1.00 bill and I will sign my name on it.

Keep it because one day it will
mean something to you. Mac
said you are so kind.

Mattress Mac contacted the television station. He told the station I want to pledge to help this lady get her magical dream.

Let her know that her house, car, and attorney fees will be paid by me.

On Christmas Day Mattress Max,
family, and staff surprised Lisa
Johnson with a blessing.

Her $1.00 dollar became over millions.

She got double for her trouble. She
kept the faith. Because through
God all things are possible!!!

Illustrator Aiden Zaire Andrews, age 13
is a very talented young artist breaking
his way through the art scene.

As a teen suffers from bullying, Miss
Lisa Johnson saw some of his drawings
and asked him to work with her on this
book project. He is now working on his
own Comic book soon to be out.

COOKING
WITHOUT HEAⅠ

Jan Morrow

Illustrated by Lynn Breeze

CONTENTS

A message for young cooks   2

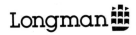
Longman

A message for young cooks

This book will help you to make lots of exciting things to eat.

Sometimes the book tells you to use a big spoon. This means a tablespoon. Ask a grown-up to show you which spoon to use.

If you need to use a knife, ask a grown-up to give you a safe one. Please be careful. Knives can be dangerous.

Remember to collect together everything you need before you start.

APPLE FIZZ

YOU WILL NEED

 apple juice

 ginger ale

 ice-cubes

 6 thin slices of red apple

 a big jug

3 glasses

1

2 glasses apple juice

1 glass ginger ale

Put the apple juice and ginger ale in the jug.

2

Put the ice-cubes in the 3 glasses.

3

Put 2 slices of apple in each glass.

4

Pour the apple fizz into the glasses.

LEMON SURPRISE

YOU
WILL
NEED

1 carton of
lemon yogurt

1 small bottle of
bitter lemon

2 slices of
lemon

a jug

2 glasses

a whisk

1

1 carton
lemon
yogurt

1 bottle
bitter
lemon

Put the yogurt and bitter
lemon in the jug.
Mix together with the whisk.

2

Pour the lemon surprise into
the glasses.

3

Put the slices of lemon in
the glasses.

BLACK COLA COOLER

YOU WILL NEED

 blackcurrant juice

 2 cans of Cola

ice-cubes

6 red cocktail cherries

3 small paper cocktail umbrellas

a jug

3 glasses

a big spoon

1

blackcurrant juice 10 spoons

Put 10 spoonfuls of blackcurrant in the jug.

2

Cola

Cola

Pour the Cola into the jug. Stir with the spoon.

3

Pour the drink into the glasses.

4

Put some ice-cubes in each glass. Put 2 cherries on each umbrella and stand the umbrellas in the glasses.

5

BANANA AND NUT MILKSHAKE

YOU WILL NEED

1 banana

1 glass of cold milk

1 small carton of hazelnut yogurt

ice-cream

a fork

a bowl

a whisk

2 glasses

an ice-cream scoop

1

Peel the banana.

Put the banana in the bowl and mash it with a fork.

2

Put the milk and yogurt in the bowl with the banana.

hazelnut yogurt

1 glass milk

Whisk together.

3

Put a scoop of ice-cream into each glass.

Put the milk shake in the glasses.

CHOCOLATE-MINT MILKSHAKE

YOU WILL NEED

chocolate ice-cream   milk   2 chocolate flakes   peppermint essence   a big bowl

a whisk   a big spoon   2 big glasses

1

1 pint milk

6 drops peppermint essence

4 spoons of chocolate ice-cream

Put the milk, peppermint and ice-cream in the bowl.

2

Whisk together.

3

Put a flake in each glass.
Put the milkshake in each glass.

A CUCUMBER CROCODILE

YOU WILL NEED 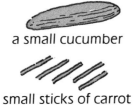 a small cucumber

small sticks of carrot

2 small cocktail onions

 2 cocktail sticks

5 triangles of cheese

 a big plate

a knife

1

Cut a thin slice from the bottom of the cucumber.

2

Cut the cucumber into 6 pieces.

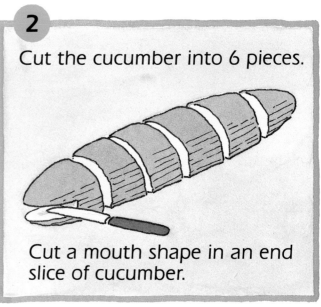

Cut a mouth shape in an end slice of cucumber.

3

Use a cocktail stick to make small holes in the mouth.

4

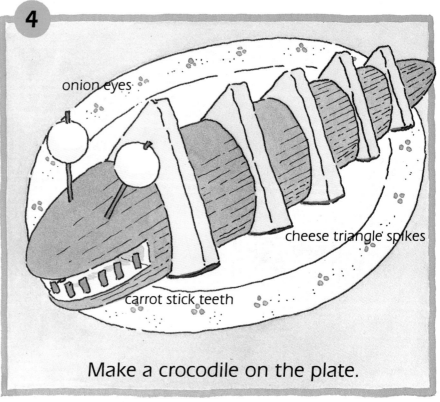

onion eyes

cheese triangle spikes

carrot stick teeth

Make a crocodile on the plate.

8

HAPPY FACE BISCUITS

YOU WILL NEED

6 plain biscuits

cream cheese
soft margarine

12 raisins
6 carrot slices

3 slices of cucumber cut in half
mustard and cress

a bowl
a big plate

a knife
a big spoon

1

3 spoonsfuls of each

Put the cream cheese and margarine in the bowl. Mix together.

2

Spread the cheese mixture on to the biscuits.

3

Make a happy face on each biscuit.

cress hair

raisin eyes

carrot nose

cucumber mouth

AN EXPRESS TRAIN TEA

YOU WILL NEED

2 slices of bread

cottage cheese

butter

6 slices of cucumber

3 slices of tomato

a big plate

a big spoon

a knife

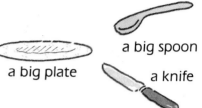

1

Butter the bread.

2

Cut the bread.

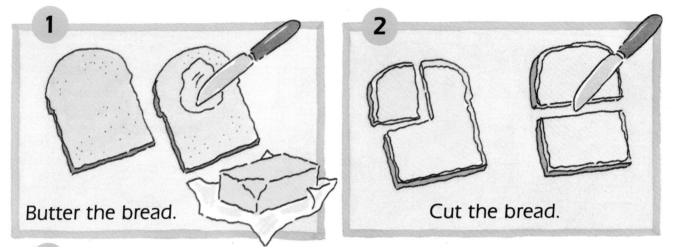

3

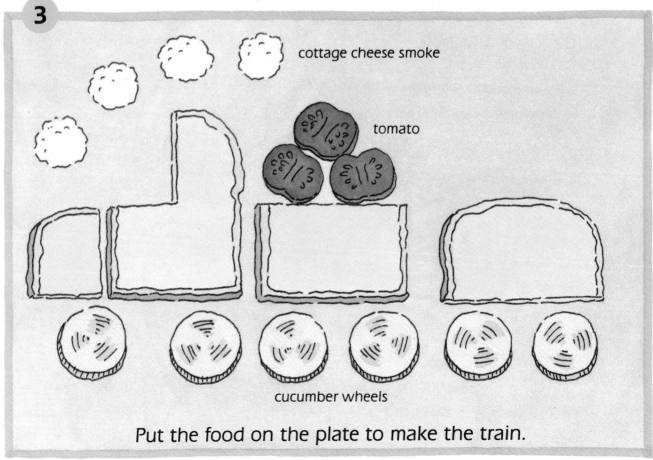

cottage cheese smoke

tomato

cucumber wheels

Put the food on the plate to make the train.

CHEESE AND FRUIT ROCKETS

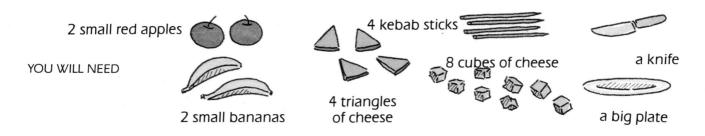

2 small red apples

YOU WILL NEED

2 small bananas

4 kebab sticks

4 triangles
of cheese

8 cubes of cheese

a knife

a big plate

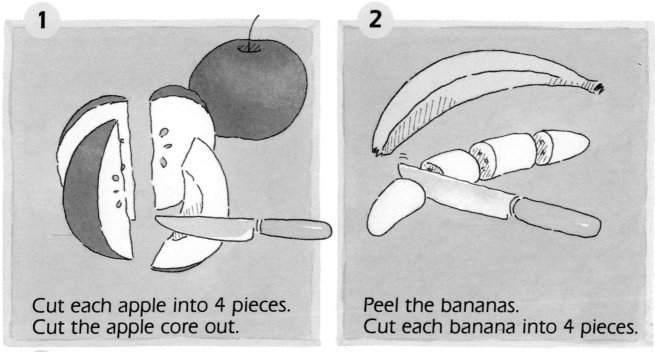

1

Cut each apple into 4 pieces.
Cut the apple core out.

2

Peel the bananas.
Cut each banana into 4 pieces.

3

Make a cheese and fruit rocket on each kebab stick.

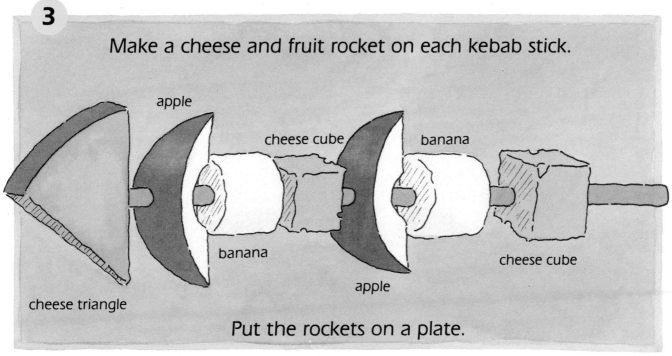

apple

cheese cube

banana

banana

apple

cheese cube

cheese triangle

Put the rockets on a plate.

11

AN UNDERWATER SUPPER

3 small bridge rolls

3 big slices of cucumber

a big plate

a knife

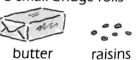

butter

raisins

a small can of sardines in tomato sauce

a bowl

a fork

1

Cut the rolls.

Cut the cucumber.

2

Butter the rolls.

3

Mash the sardines.

4

Put the sardines on the rolls.

5

raisin eyes

cucumber tails

Put the rolls on the plate and make some little fish.

EGG MICE

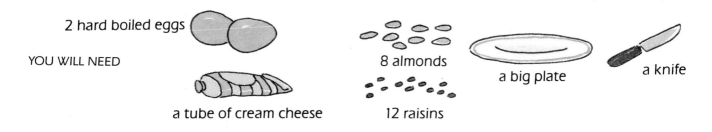

YOU WILL NEED

2 hard boiled eggs

a tube of cream cheese

8 almonds

12 raisins

a big plate

a knife

1

Take the shells off the eggs.

2

Cut each egg in half.

3

Put the food on the plate and make a mouse.

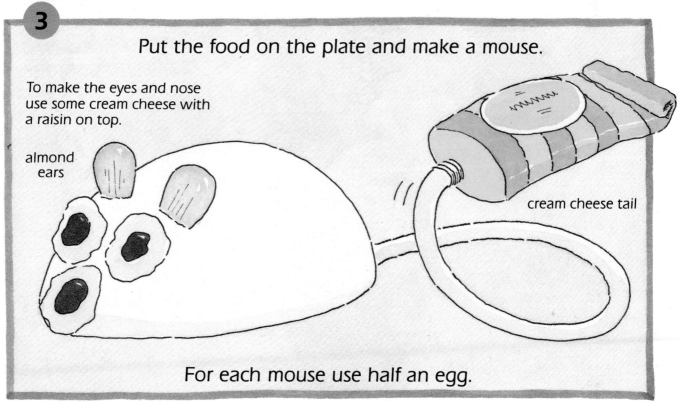

To make the eyes and nose use some cream cheese with a raisin on top.

almond ears

cream cheese tail

For each mouse use half an egg.

A LION'S FACE SALAD

YOU WILL NEED

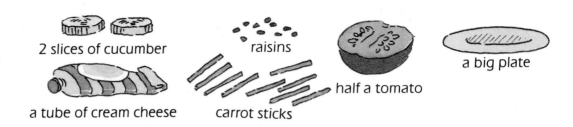

2 slices of cucumber

a tube of cream cheese

carrot sticks

raisins

half a tomato

a big plate

a carrot stick and cheese curl mane

cucumber eyes

a tomato nose

raisin whiskers

a cream cheese mouth

Make a lion's face on the plate.

PEANUT FUDGE SUNDAE

YOU WILL NEED

honey

peanut butter

raisins

vanilla ice-cream

a bowl

water

a big spoon

2 big glasses

1

honey 2 spoons

peanut butter 2 spoons

water 1 spoon

Make a peanut sauce.
Mix the peanut butter, honey and water.

2

raisins

ice-cream

peanut sauce

raisins

ice-cream

peanut sauce

Put the peanut sauce, ice-cream and raisins in the big glasses.

15

ICE-CREAM WITCHES

YOU WILL NEED

2 ice-cream cones

vanilla ice-cream

2 chocolate biscuits

Smarties

2 small plates

an ice-cream scoop

1

Put one biscuit on each plate.

Put a scoop of ice-cream on each biscuit.

2

Press a cone hat on to the ice-cream.

3

Make a witch. Make the eyes and nose from Smarties.

WHITE RABBITS

YOU
WILL
NEED

 a bowl of
green jelly

 tinned
pears

 almonds

glacé
cherries

 a can of squirt cream

 a fork

 small bowls

1

Mash the jelly with the fork.

2

Put some jelly in each bowl.
Put half a pear on top of
the jelly.

3

almond ears

a squirt cream tail

Make the eyes and
nose from cherries.

Use the almonds, cherries and cream to make a white rabbit.

A FIELD FULL OF MUSHROOMS

YOU WILL NEED

small meringue shells

grated chocolate

marshmallows

a bowl of green jelly

a big plate

a fork

1 Mash the jelly with the fork.

2 Put the jelly on to the plate.

3

Sprinkle with grated chocolate.

meringue shell mushroom tops

marshmallow stalks

Make the mushrooms.

BANANA BUTTERFLY CUSTARD

YOU WILL NEED

cold custard

a peeled banana

2 glacé cherries

2 fan shaped wafer biscuits

2 cocktail sticks

a big plate

a big spoon

1

Spoon some custard on to the plate.

2

Put the banana in the middle of the custard.

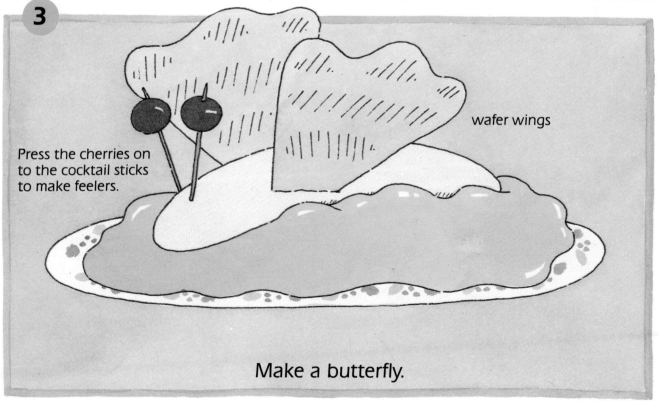

3

Press the cherries on to the cocktail sticks to make feelers.

wafer wings

Make a butterfly.

KITTEN CAKES

YOU WILL NEED

 icing sugar

 cocoa powder

 swiss roll

 milk

Smarties

jelly diamonds

chocolate sticks

butter

 a bowl

a knife

 a big spoon

a big plate

1

Make some chocolate cream.

icing sugar 8 spoons

milk 1 spoon

cocoa powder 2 spoons

butter 4 spoons

Mix together.

2

Cut the swiss roll into slices.

3

Put the chocolate cream on to the swiss roll slices.

4

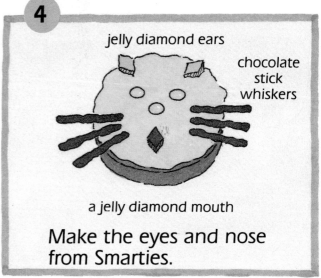

jelly diamond ears

chocolate stick whiskers

a jelly diamond mouth

Make the eyes and nose from Smarties.

EASTER BONNETS

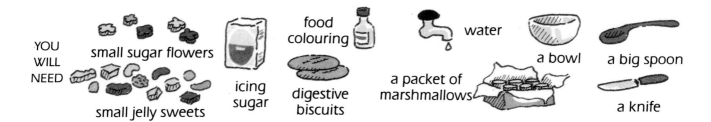

YOU WILL NEED — small sugar flowers, small jelly sweets, icing sugar, food colouring, digestive biscuits, water, a packet of marshmallows, a bowl, a big spoon, a knife

1

icing sugar 4 spoons

food colouring 2 drops

water 1 spoon

Make some coloured icing.

2

Spread the icing on to the biscuits.

3

Put a marshmallow in the middle of each biscuit.

4

Put the small sweets and flowers round the marshmallow.

CHOCOLATE HEDGEHOGS

YOU WILL NEED

 icing sugar milk cocoa powder

margarine

 chocolate buns

chocolate buttons

glacé cherries

sugar silver balls

 a bowl

 a big spoon

a knife

1

Make some chocolate cream.

icing sugar 8 spoons

cocoa powder 2 spoons

margarine 4 spoons

milk 1 spoon

Mix together.

2

Turn the buns upside down.

Put the chocolate cream on the buns.

3

Make the hedgehogs.

silver ball eyes

a glacé cherry nose

chocolate button spines

22

A MARZIPAN MONSTER

YOU WILL NEED

butter
cake crumbs
caster sugar
almond essence
jelly diamonds
2 raisins
a glacé cherry
green food colouring
a clean paint brush
string
a bowl
a big spoon

1

butter 2 spoons

caster sugar 2 spoons

Mix together.

2

almond essence 4 drops

cake crumbs 8 spoons

Mix together the cake crumbs and almond essence with the butter and sugar.

3

raisin eyes

jelly diamonds.

Paint the monster with the green food colouring.

cherry nose

Use this marzipan to make a monster.

string tail

SUGAR MICE

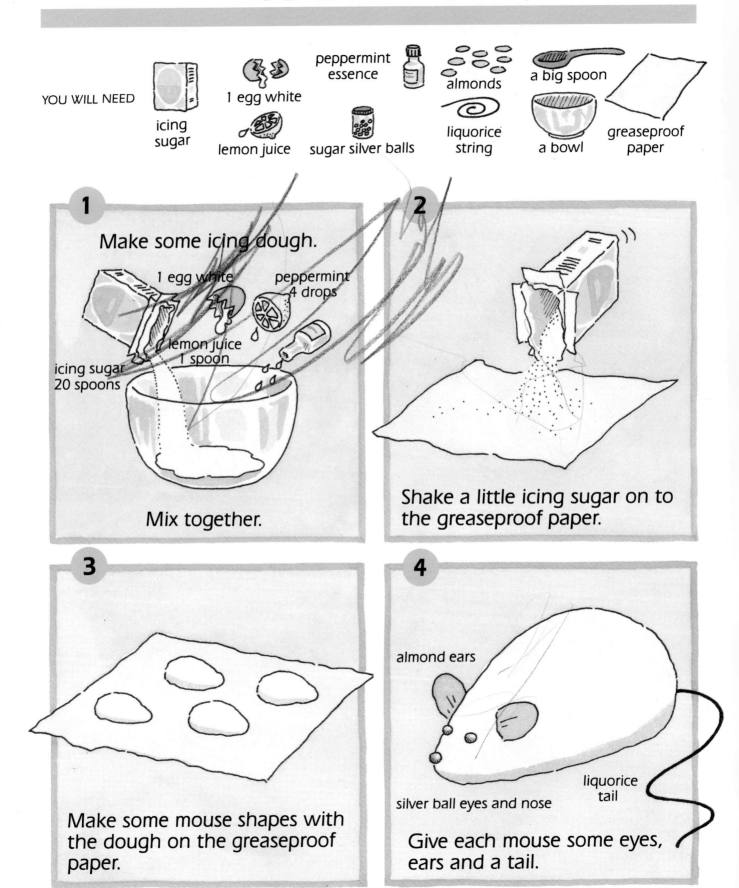

YOU WILL NEED

icing sugar

1 egg white

lemon juice

peppermint essence

sugar silver balls

almonds

liquorice string

a big spoon

a bowl

greaseproof paper

1

Make some icing dough.

1 egg white

peppermint 4 drops

lemon juice 1 spoon

icing sugar 20 spoons

Mix together.

2

Shake a little icing sugar on to the greaseproof paper.

3

Make some mouse shapes with the dough on the greaseproof paper.

4

almond ears

silver ball eyes and nose

liquorice tail

Give each mouse some eyes, ears and a tail.